Topic: Interpersonal Skills **Subtopic:** Empathy

Note to Parents and Teachers:
Children enter school with a vast understanding of spoken language, but written letters and words are not as familiar. The best way to get children reading is to teach them how to decode words. Begin by teaching that words are made up of phonemes (sounds). Then, teach children the letters that stand for those phonemes. As their decoding abilities get stronger, they will begin to comprehend what they are reading as well. These skills will help them become proficient readers.

Bookends for the Reader!

Here are some reminders before reading the text:
- Look through the pages of the book to get a sense of the story and make a connection to something you already know.
- Focus on letter sounds instead of letter names. Practice sounding out each word letter by letter (sound by sound) and blending the sounds to read words.
- Some words may need to be memorized because they are not decodable.

Words to Know Before You Read

adventure
explore
forest
friends
laugh
shadows
walk
werewolf

How to Be Friends with This Werewolf

By Erin Savory
Illustrated by Ana Zurita

Rourke

I met Walda in the forest.

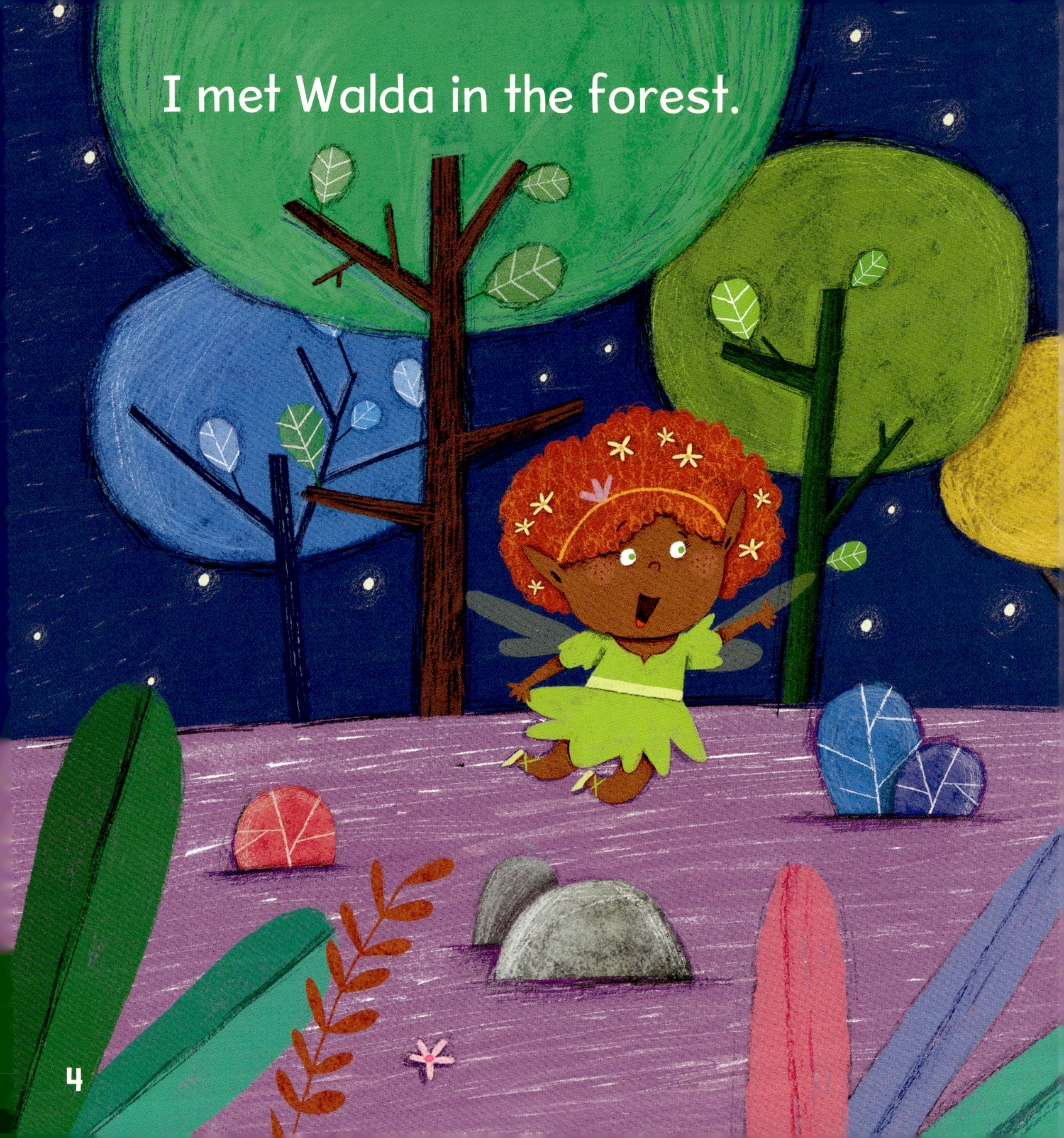

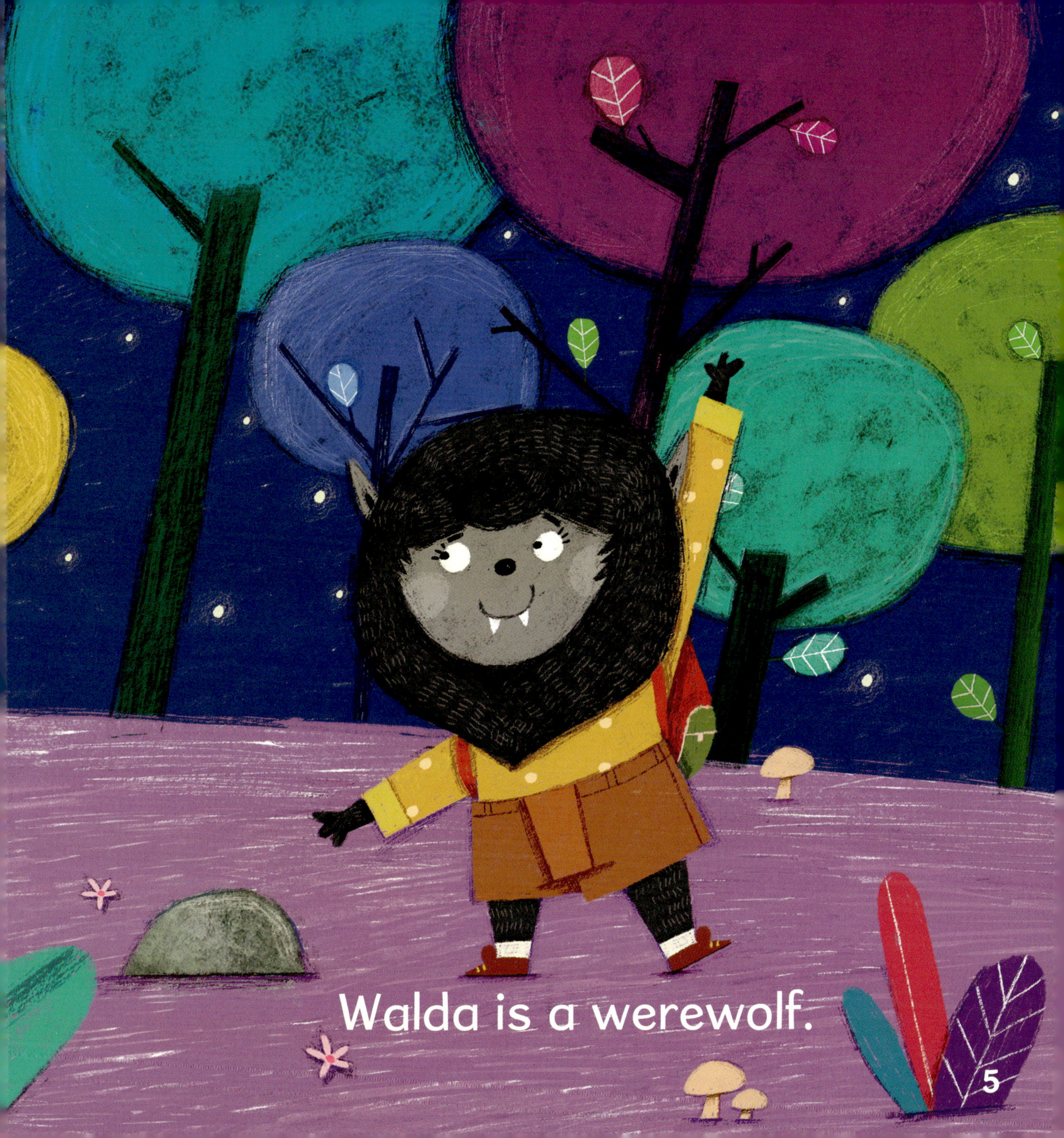

Walda is a werewolf.

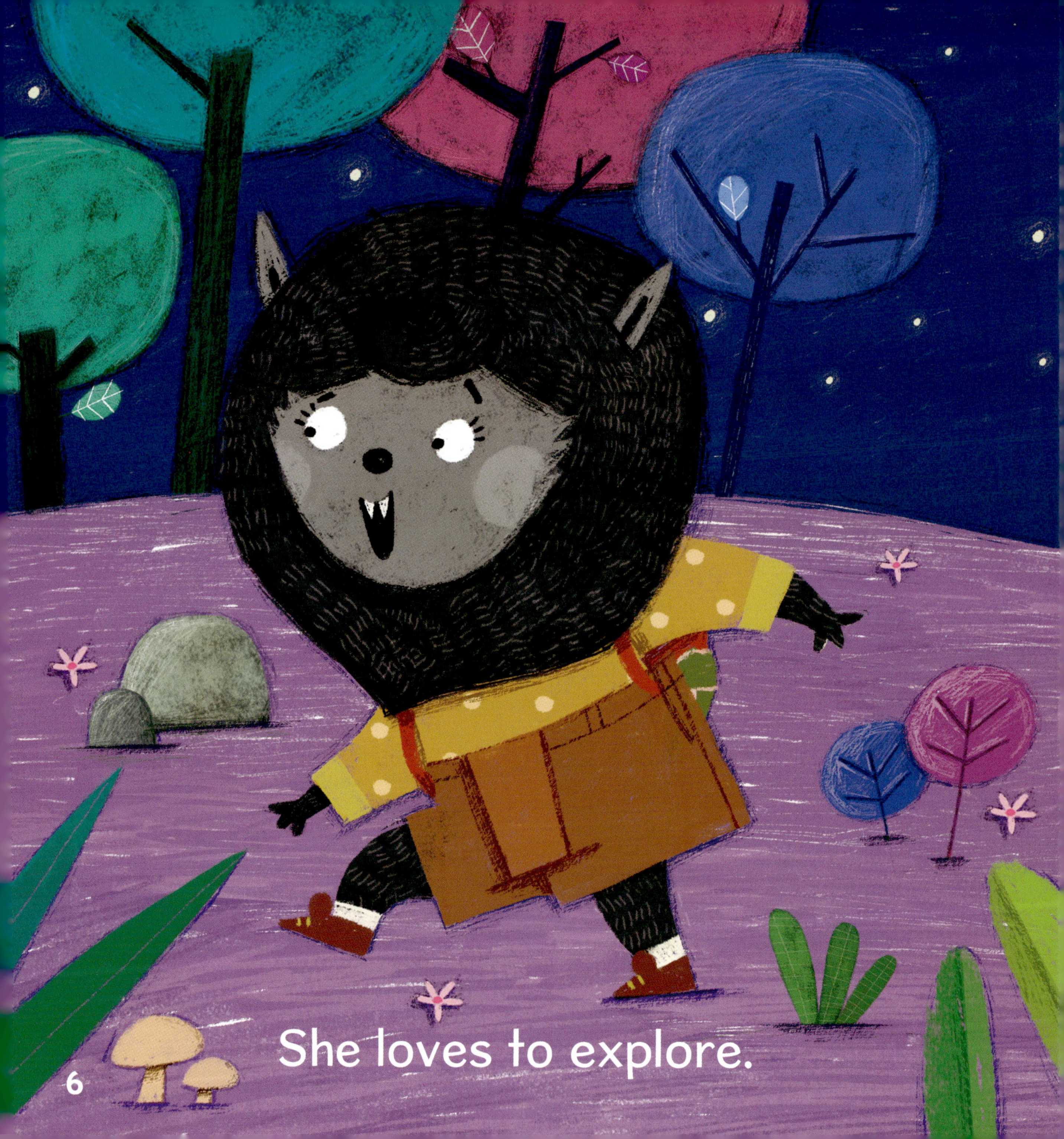

She loves to explore.

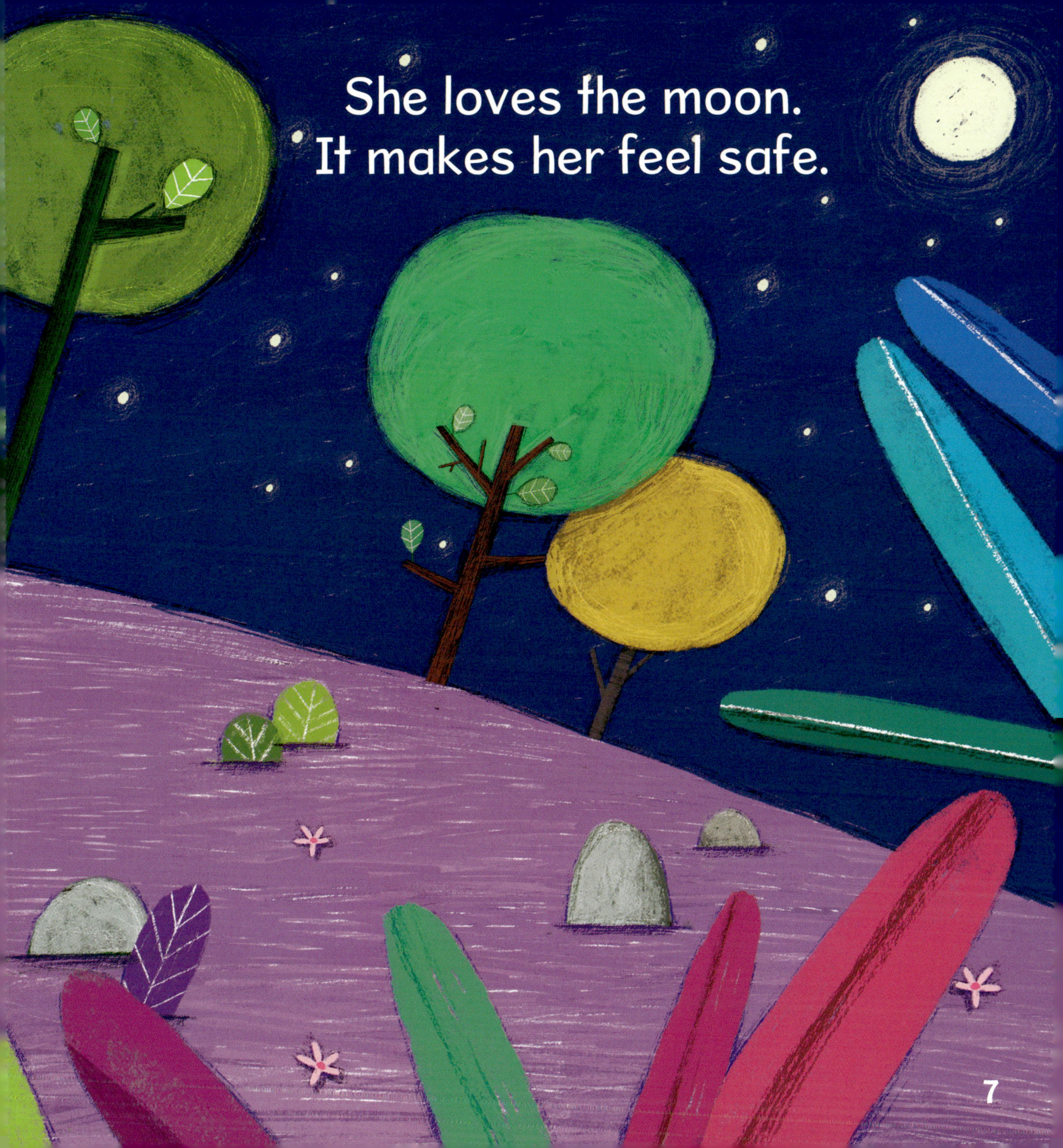

She loves the moon.
It makes her feel safe.

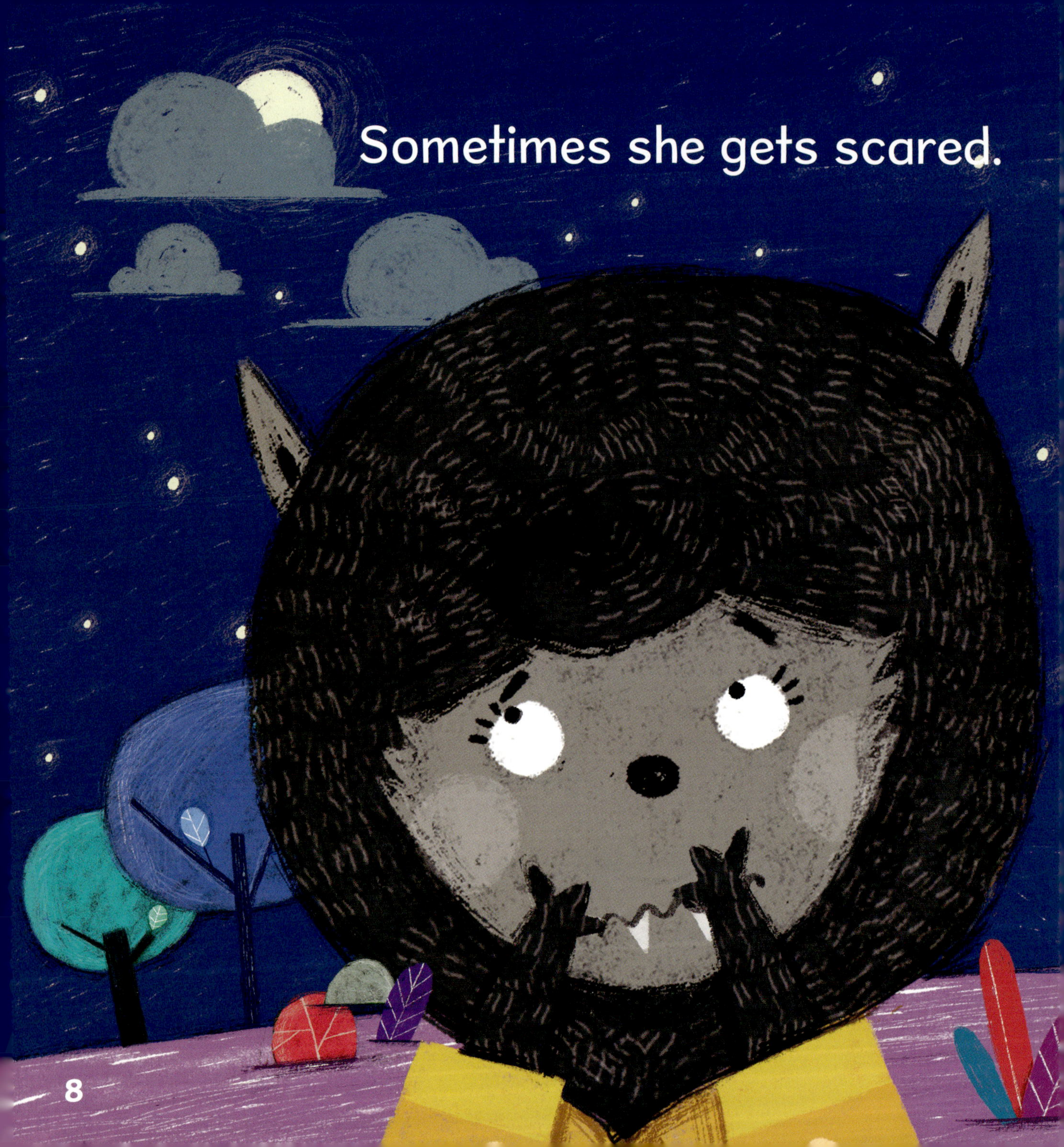

Sometimes she gets scared.

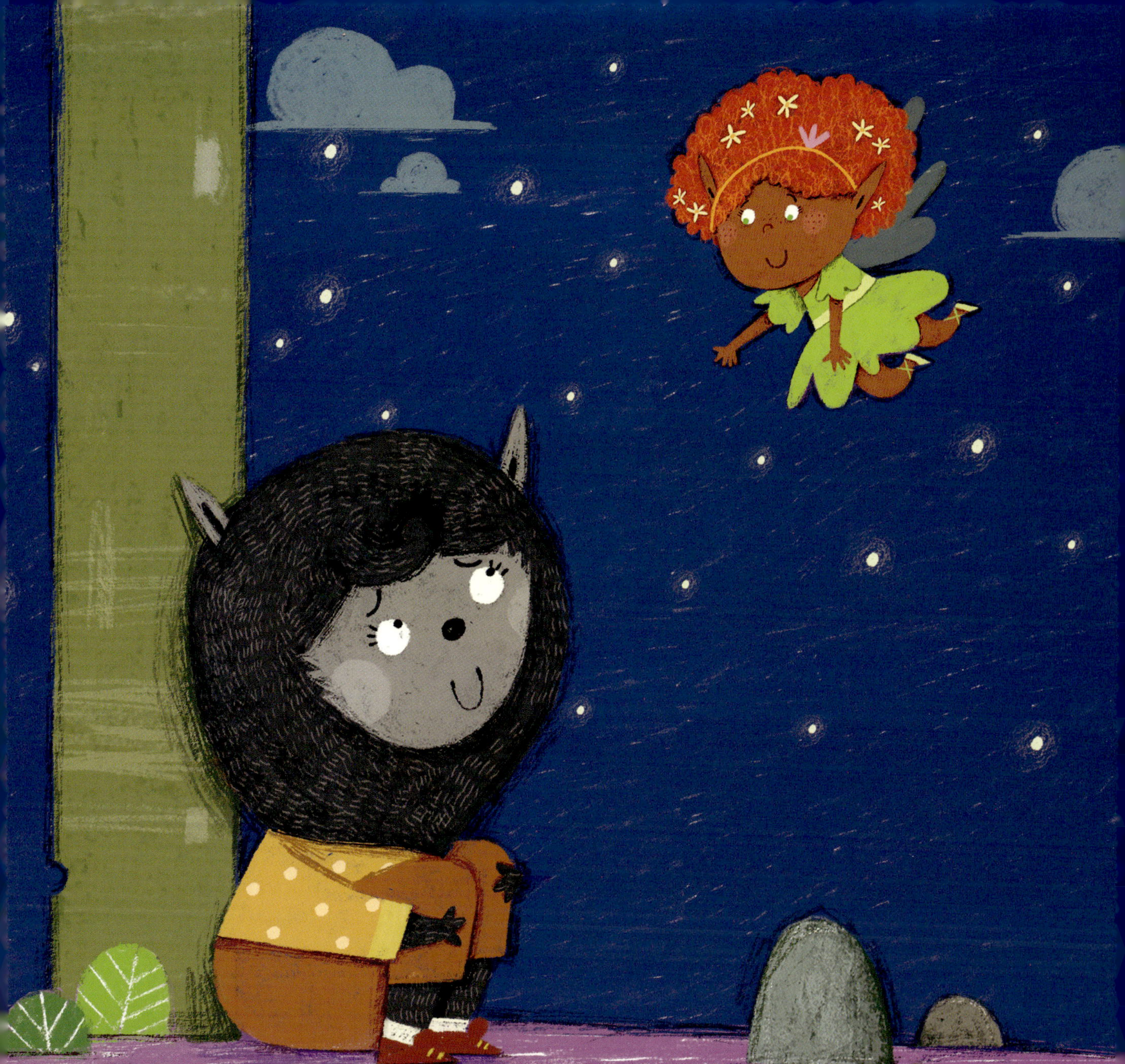

How can I be friends with this werewolf?

We explore together.
We use our maps.

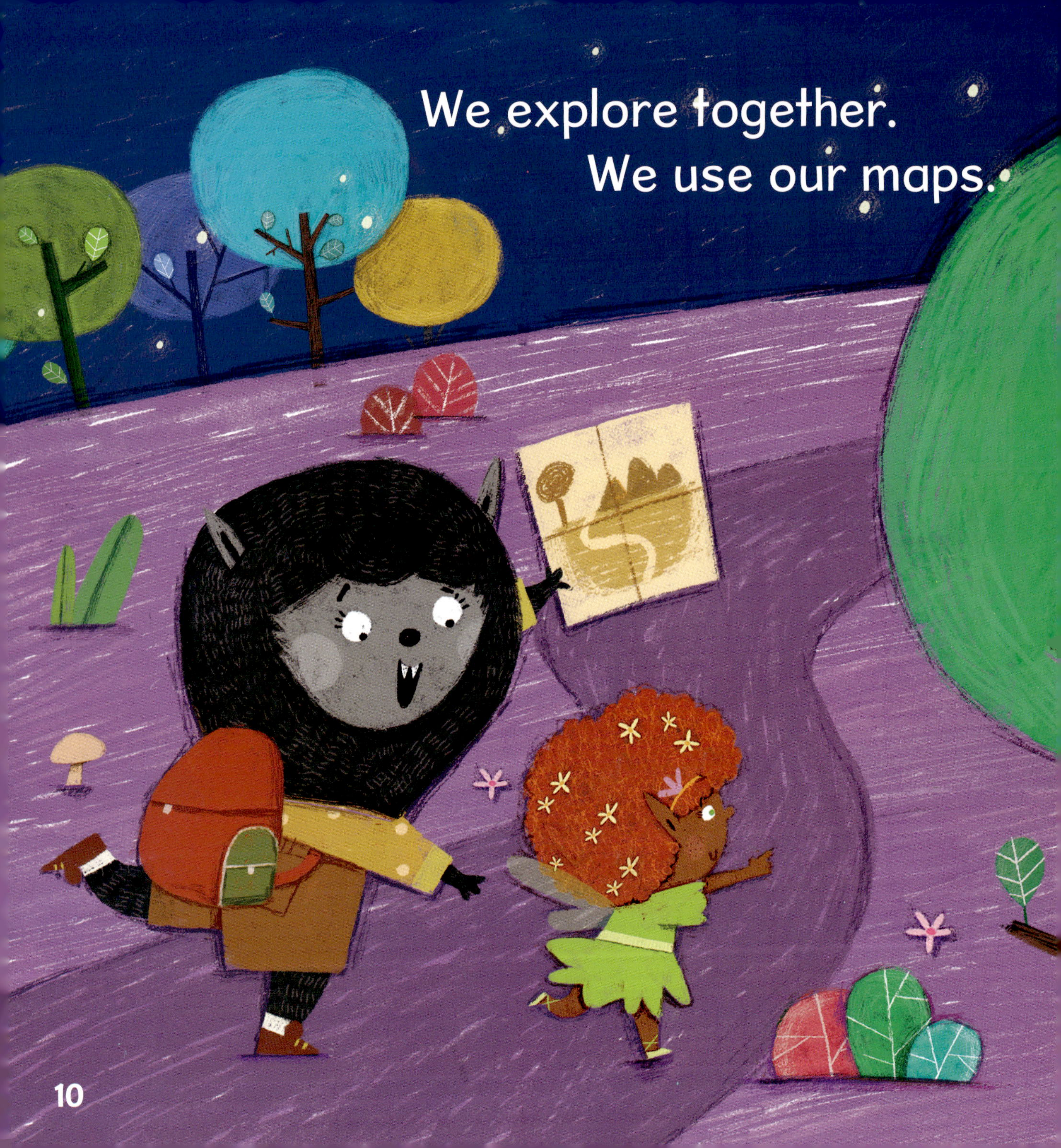

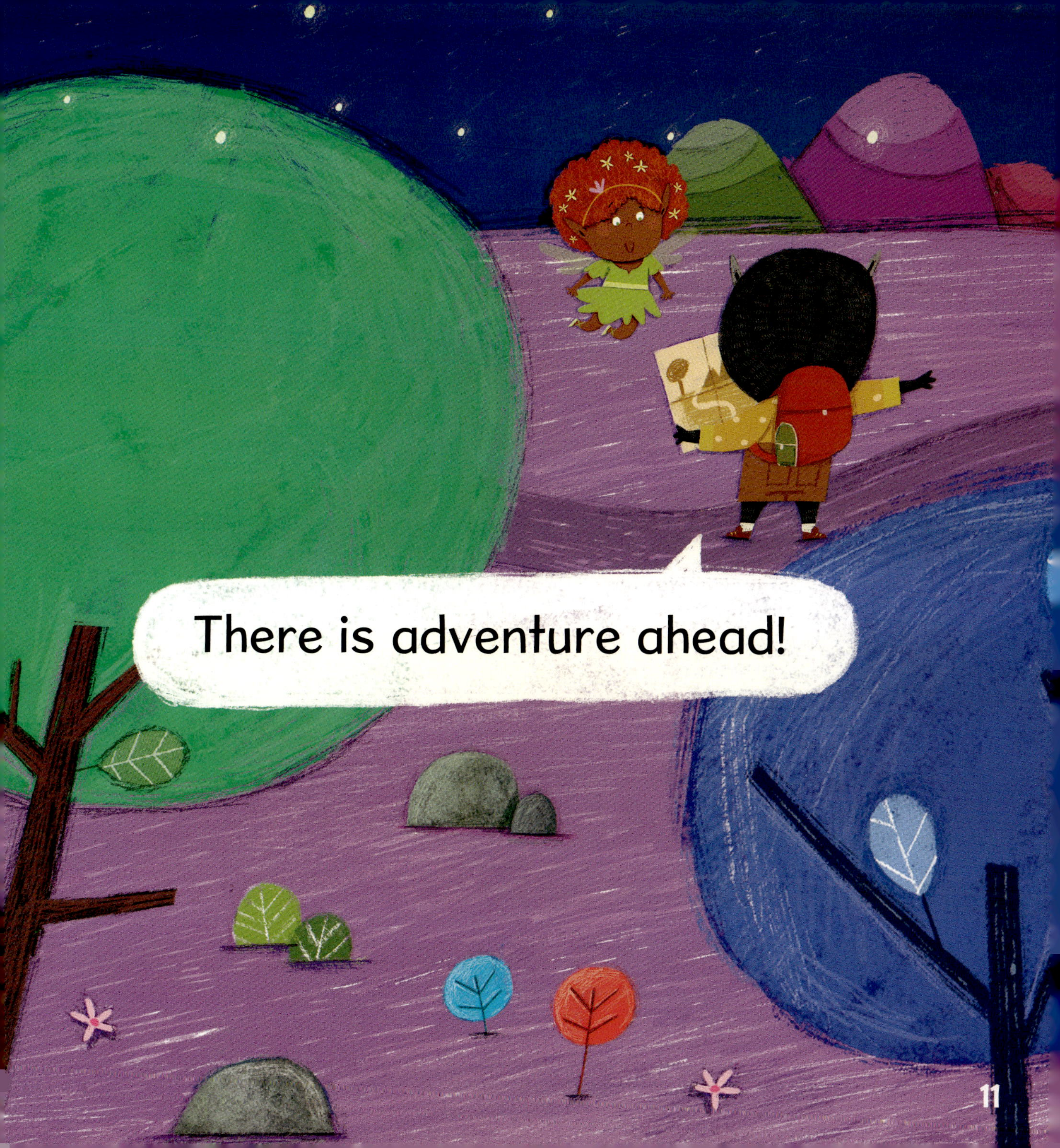
There is adventure ahead!

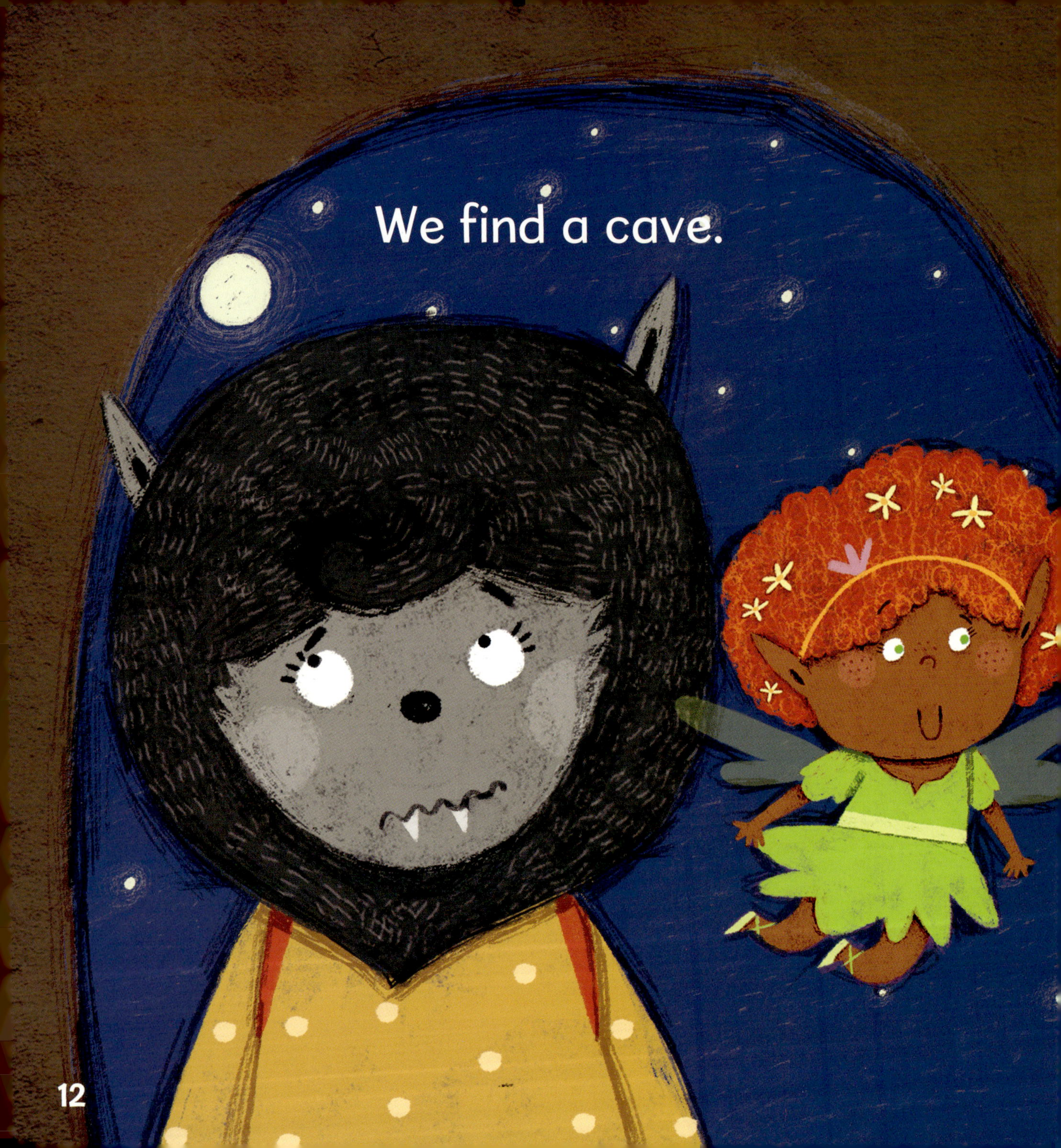

We find a cave.

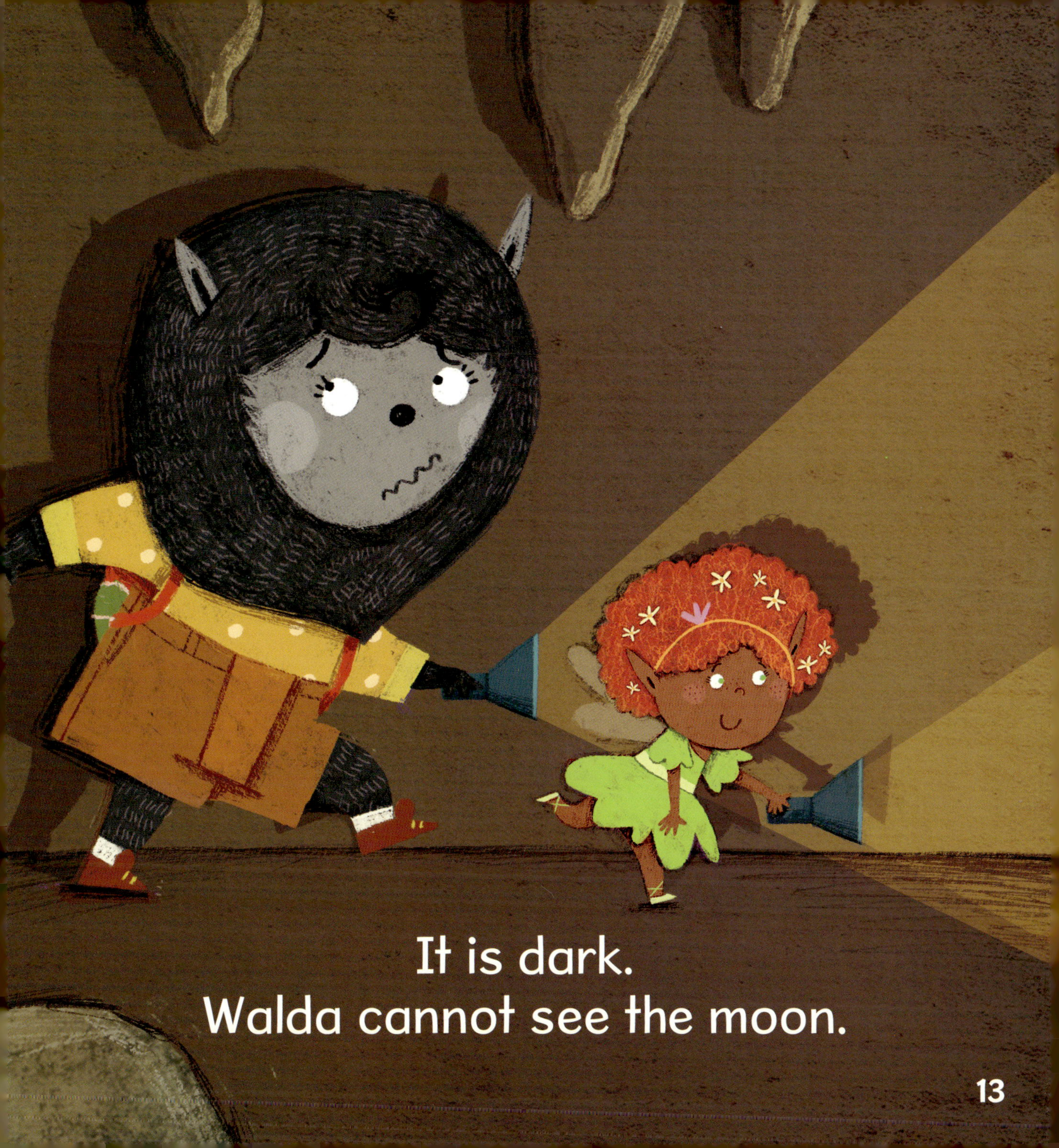

It is dark.
Walda cannot see the moon.

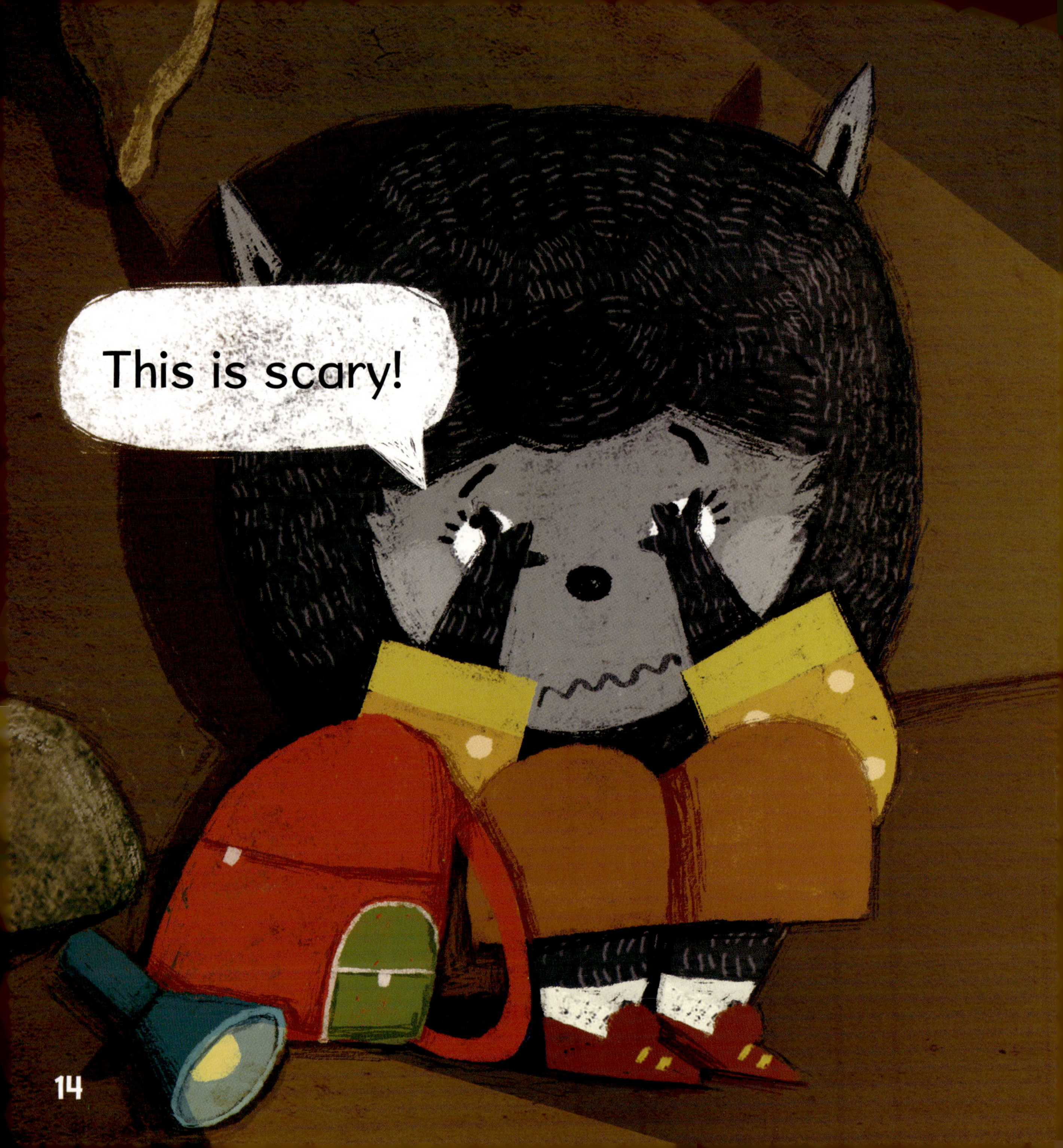
This is scary!

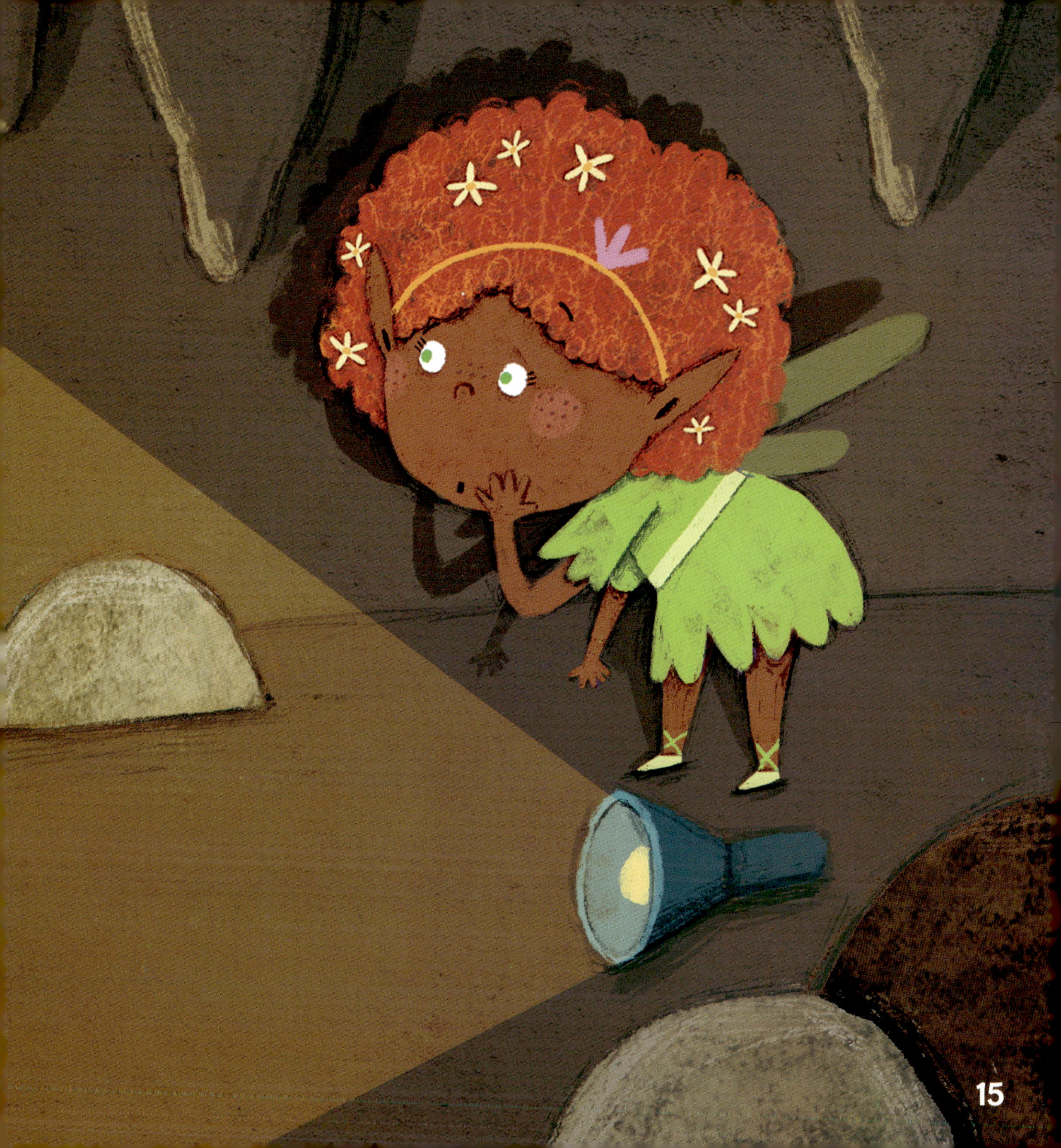

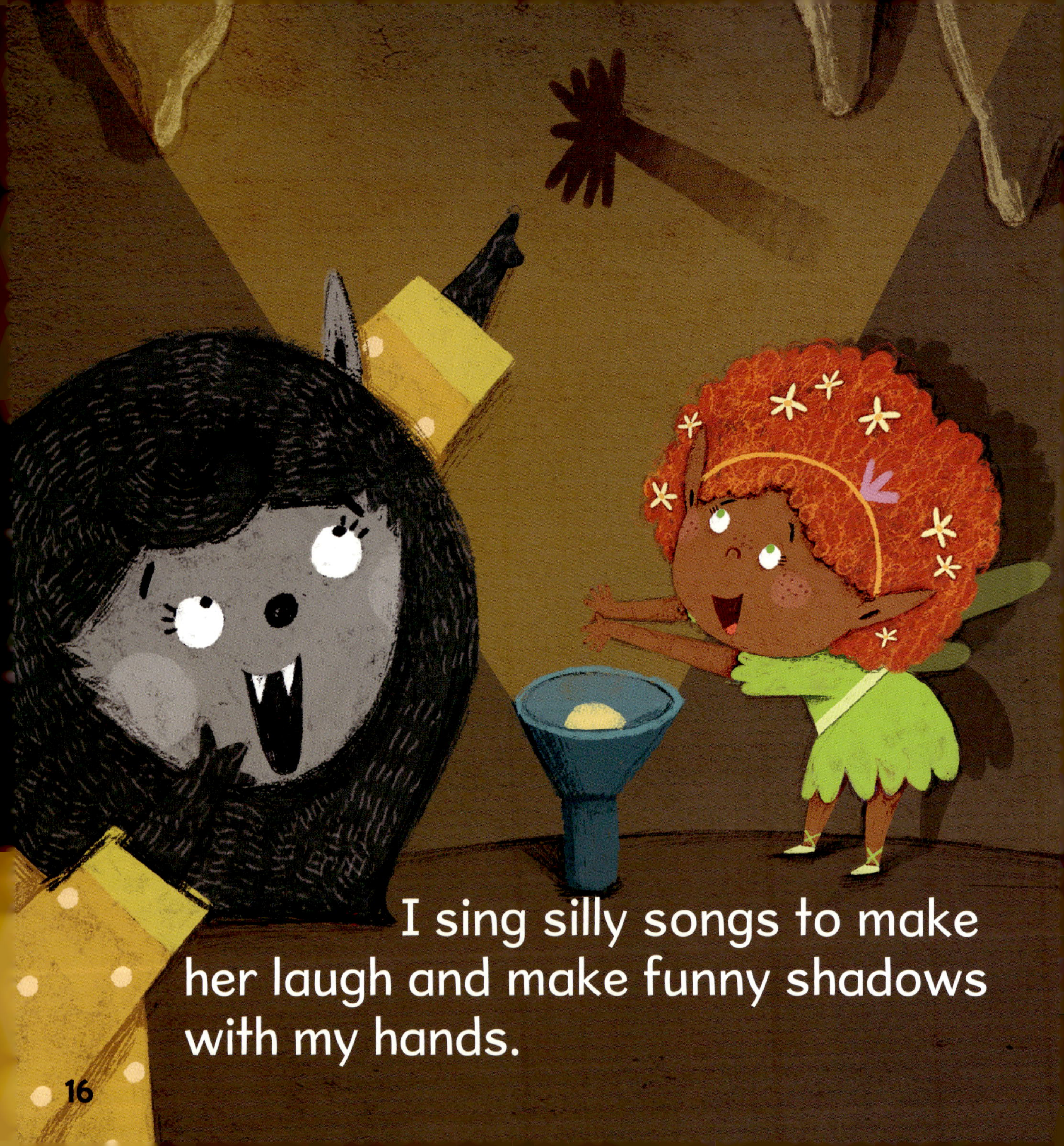

I sing silly songs to make her laugh and make funny shadows with my hands.

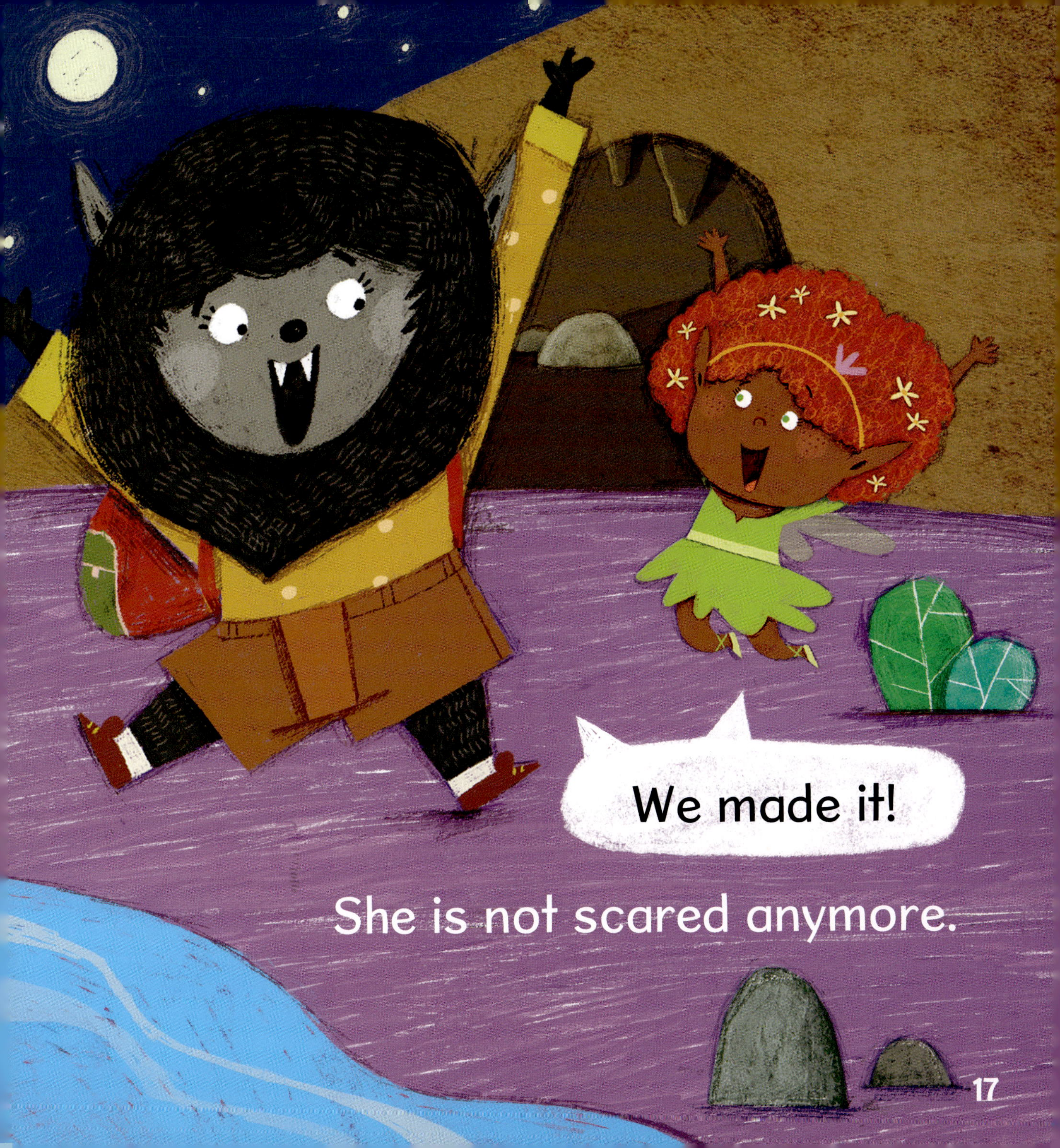
We made it!

She is not scared anymore.

We walk to a river.

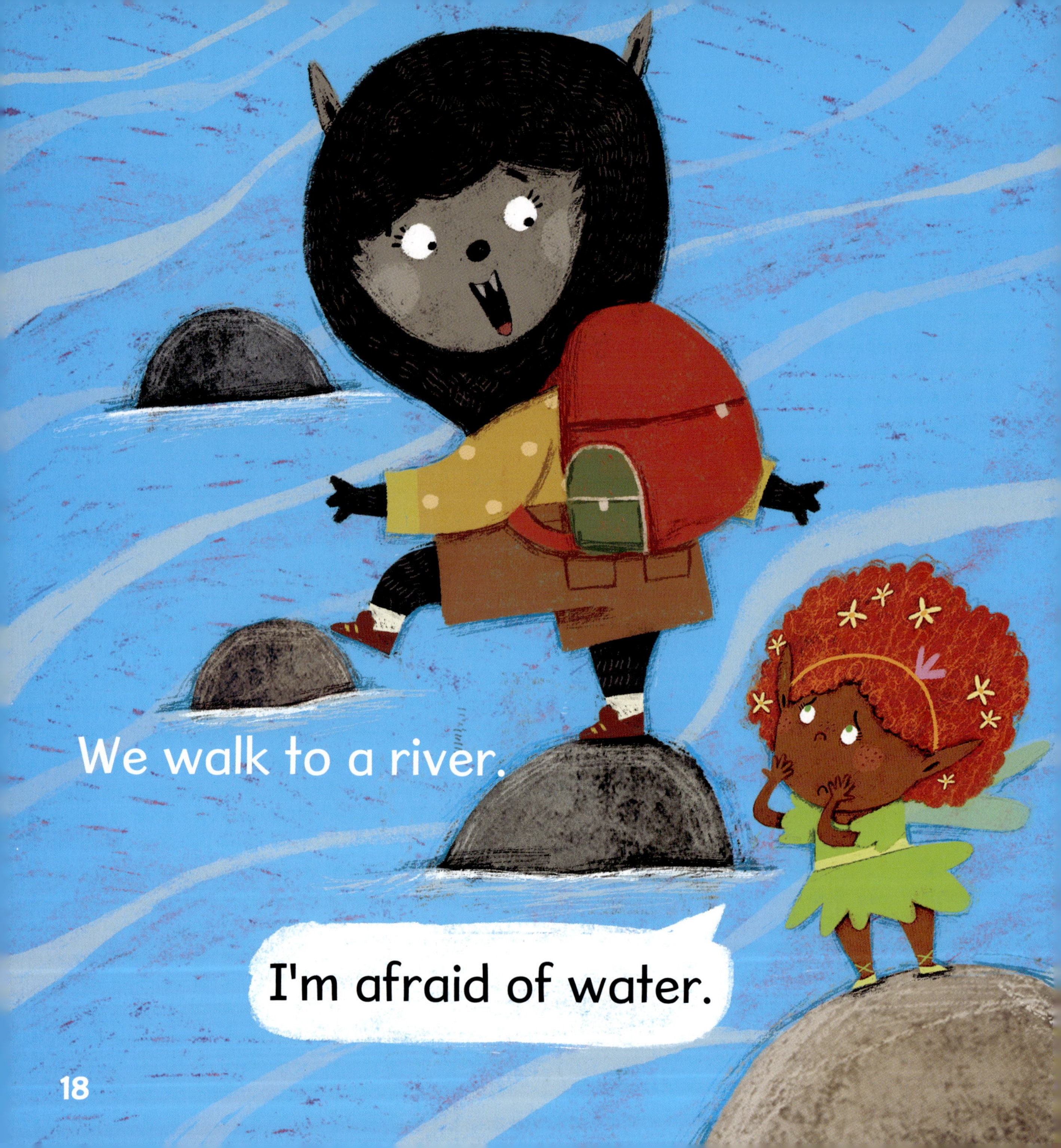
I'm afraid of water.

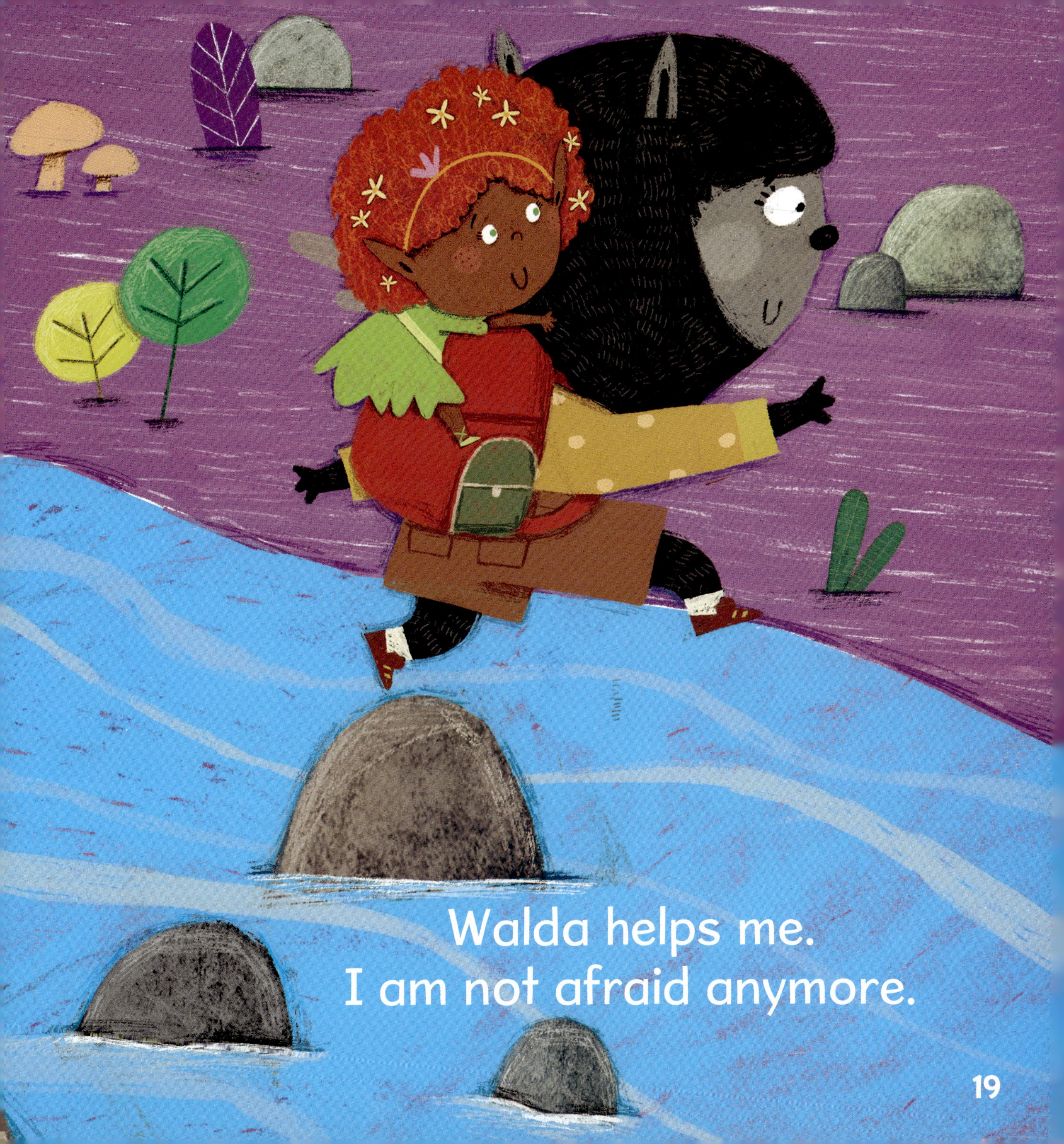

Walda helps me.
I am not afraid anymore.

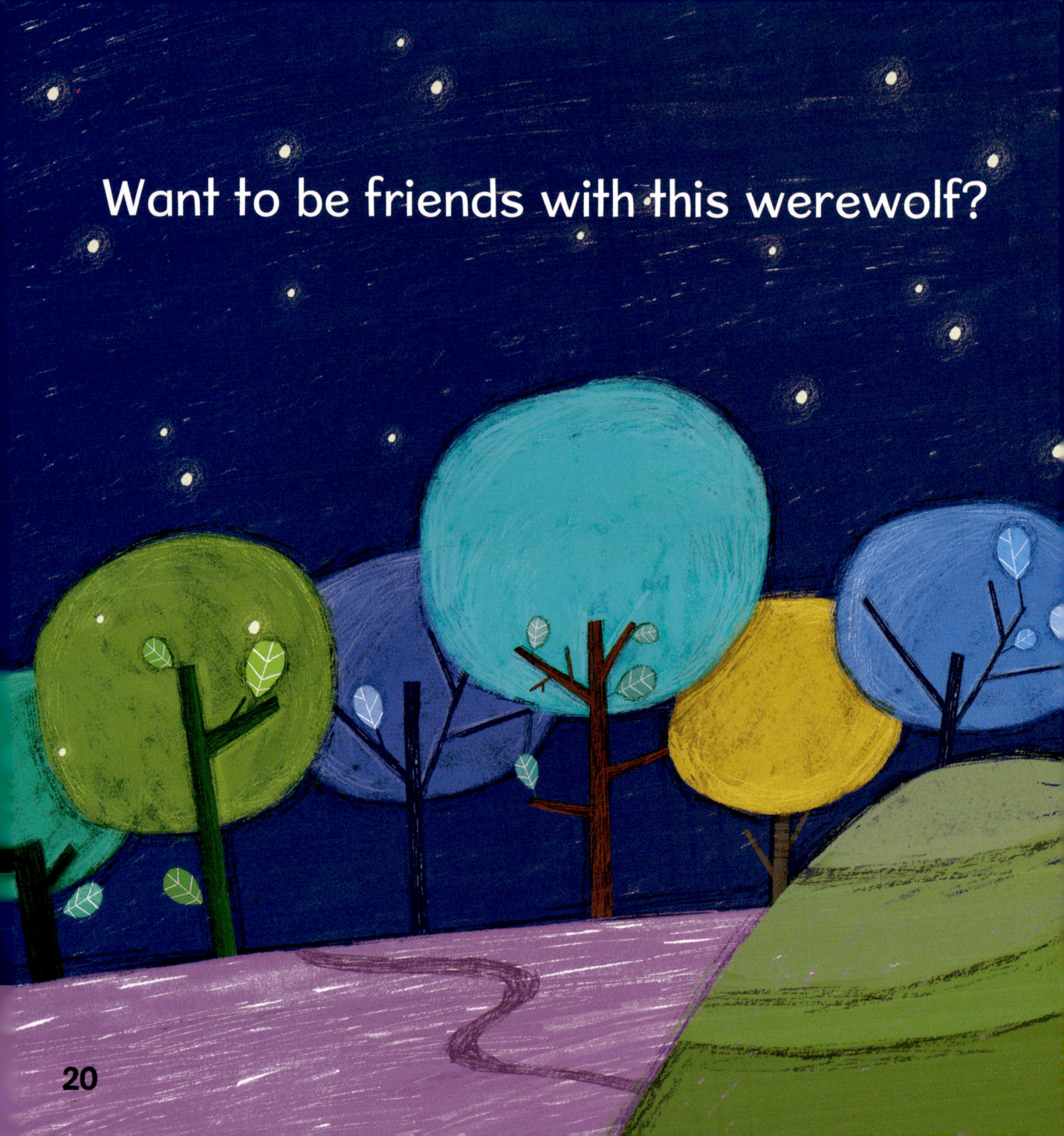

Want to be friends with this werewolf?

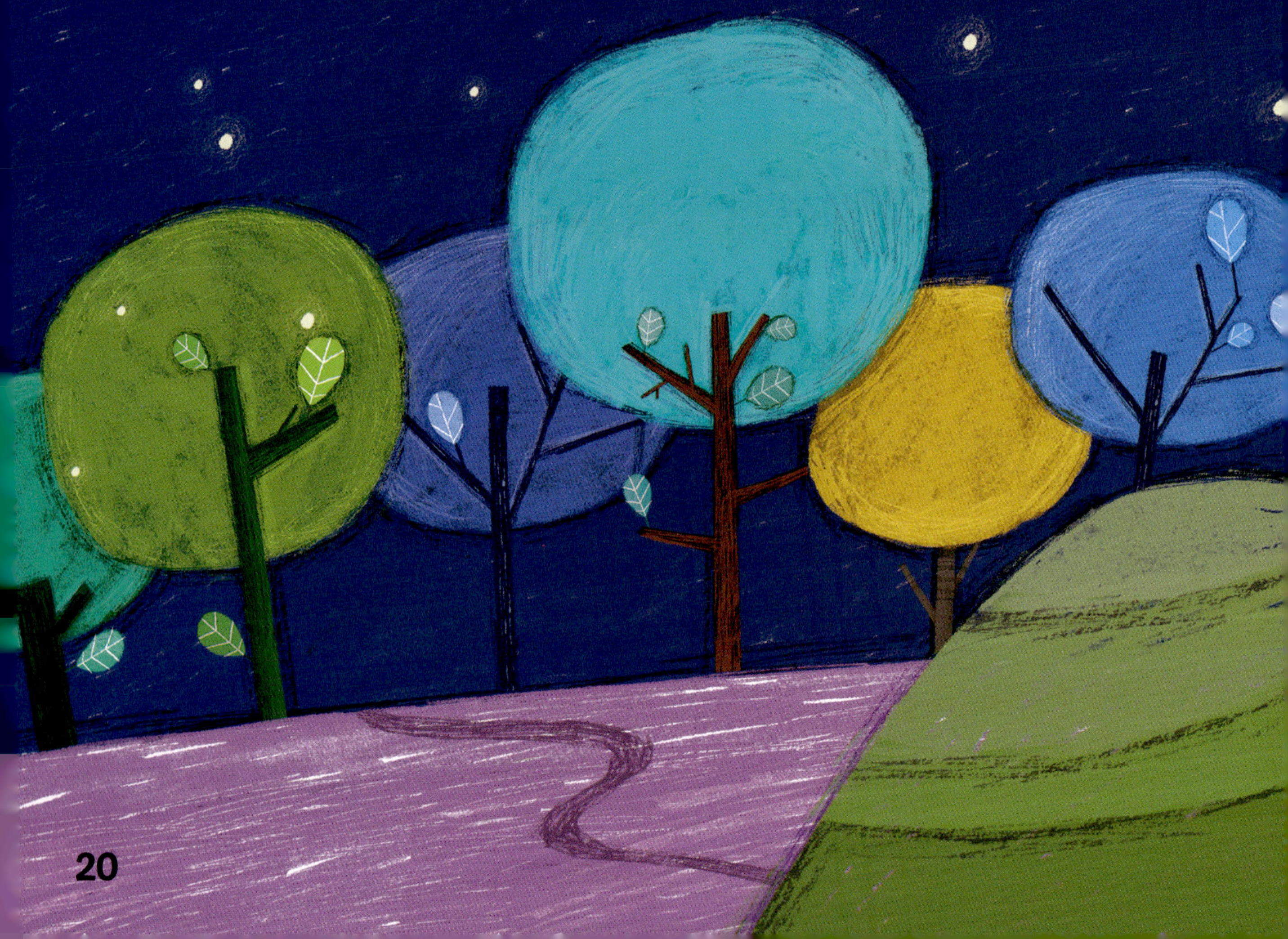

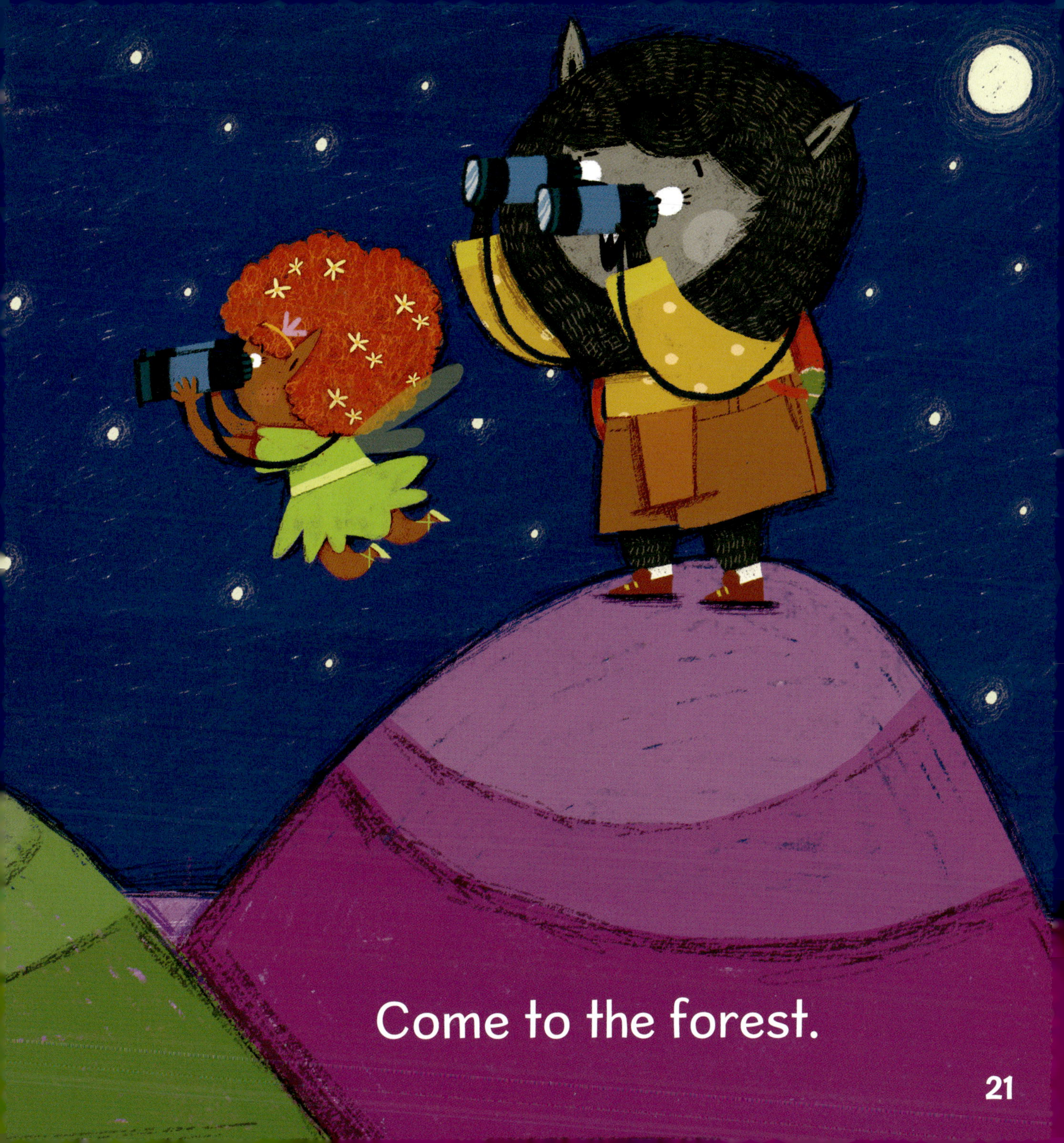

Come to the forest.

Walda is ready for adventure!

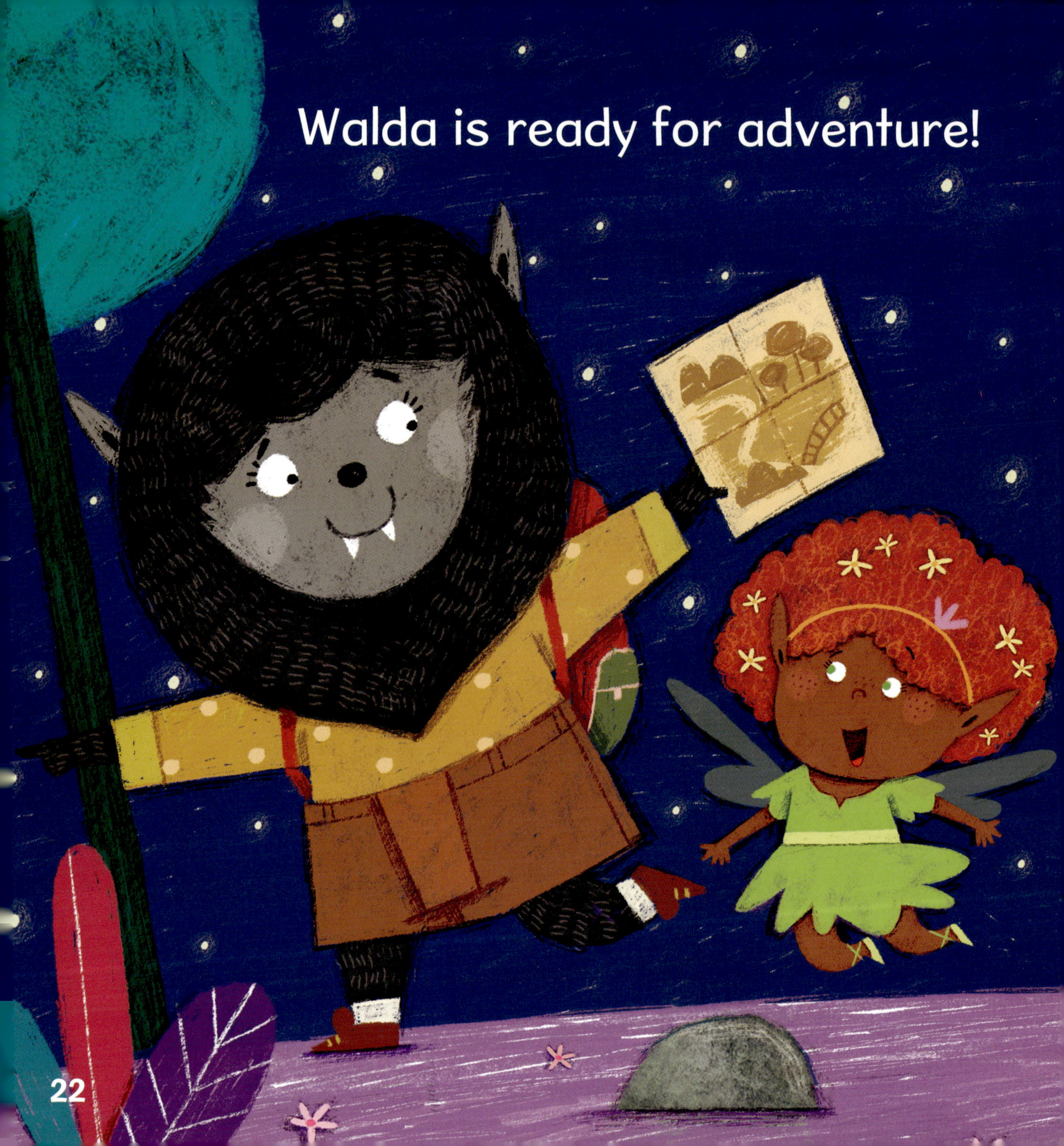

Bookends for the Reader

"I know..."
What does Walda like to do?

"I think..."
How does Walda help when her friend is scared?

What happened in this book?
Look at each picture and talk about what happened in the story.

About the Author

Erin Savory is a writer who lives in Florida. She loves to paint with her two-year-old son. She loves spending time in nature. Reading is her favorite activity.

About the Illustrator

Ana Zurita was born by the sea in Valencia, Spain, where she completed her studies in Fine Arts and currently lives with her wonderful family. She is a big fan of the beach in winter, the color yellow, the smell of old books, and heavy blankets. But what has made her the happiest from a very early age is drawing. That's why her greatest dream is to make others happy with her illustrations.

Library of Congress PCN Data

How to Be Friends with This Werewolf / Erin Savory
(How to Be Friends)
ISBN 978-1-73164-347-6 (hard cover)
ISBN 978-1-73164-311-7 (soft cover)
ISBN 978-1-73164-379-7 (e-Book)
ISBN 978-1-73164-411-4 (ePub)
Library of Congress Control Number: 2020945146

Rourke Educational Media
Printed in Ningbo, Zhejiang, China
08-0202512936

© 2021 Rourke Educational Media

All rights reserved. No part of this book may be reproduced or utilized in any form or by any means, electronic or mechanical including photocopying, recording, or by any information storage and retrieval system without permission in writing from the publisher.

www.rourkebooks.com

Edited by: Tracie Santos
Layout by: Morgan Burnside
Cover and interior illustrations by: Ana Zurita